Where Are You, Puffling?

An Irish Adventure

RE-TOLD BY **Erika McGann**

FROM A STORY BY **Sean Daly**

ILLUSTRATIONS BY **Gerry Daly**

THE O'BRIEN PRESS

DUBLIN

The sun was coming up over Skellig Michael.

A little puffling popped her head out of her burrow.

'What a lovely day!' she said.

'It's a perfect day to have an adventure.'

The puffling stretched her wings
and shook her fluffy, black feathers.

She walked through the grass,

across the path,

past the rocks,

and over the hill.

Two puffin parents were worried. Their burrow was empty, and they couldn't see their puffling anywhere.

'Where are you, puffling?' they called.

'I saw a puffling,' said a gannet nearby.

'She helped me fix my nest.

'Someone stood on it and left a big bootprint.

The puffling collected weeds and twigs, and covered it up.

She is very quick and very clever.'

'Which way did she go?' the puffins asked.

'That way,' said the gannet. 'Towards that big rock.'

9

'Where are you, puffling?' the puffins called.

'I saw a puffling,' said a rabbit nearby.

'She helped me dig a burrow.

'I hurt my paw, you see, so she dug the burrow for me.

What an excellent digger that puffling is.'

'Did you see which way she went?' asked the puffins.

'That way,' said the rabbit. 'Towards those stone huts.'

'Where are you, puffling?' the puffins cried out.

'I saw a puffling,' said a kittiwake chick nearby.
'She helped me find my parents.

'I lost them in a rock fall. The puffling hopped up onto the
rocks and there they were! She is such a clever bird.'

'Where did she go after that?' asked the puffins.

'That way,' said the kittiwake chick.

'Towards the cliff.'

'Where are you, puffling?' shouted the puffins.

'I saw a puffling,' said a dolphin nearby.
'She helped me catch some fish.

'She spotted the fish from the cliff, like shadows in the water.
She told me where they were. What good eyesight she has.'

'But where did she go?' the puffins asked.

'That way,' said the dolphin. 'Towards the cove.'

'Where are you, puffling?' yelled the puffins.

'I saw a puffling,' said a seal nearby.
'She helped me when I was stuck.

'My foot got caught in some plastic, and she snipped it with her sharp beak. She is a kind little puffling.'

'Please tell us where she went,' said the puffins.

'That way,' said the seal. 'Towards the jetty.'

'Where are you, puffling?' the puffins called.

'Mummy, Daddy, I'm over here!' cried the puffling.

The puffling stood on the deck of a boat
... that was sailing out to sea!

'I can't fly yet,' the puffling sniffed, flapping her tiny wings. 'Please come and take me home!'

But the puffling was too heavy for the puffins to carry.
So they came up with a plan.

'Don't worry, puffling, we'll get you home!'

The puffins called out to the seal, and the seal wriggled away on her belly.

The seal cried out to the kittiwake chick,
and the chick scurried up the hill.

The kittiwake chick chirped to the rabbit,
and the rabbit hopped over the path.

The rabbit hollered to the gannet in the sky,
and the gannet dove into the ocean.

The gannet whispered to the dolphin,
and the dolphin raced through the water.

Deep, deep down,
there were the whales ...

'**What is this?**' the puffling cried,
as the boat rose up out of the water.

'**We're taking you home, little puffling,**' said the whales.

'Your parents asked for help.'

And so the puffling floated home
on a boat that sailed on the backs of whales.

The sun was setting over Skellig Michael.

Safe in her burrow, a little puffling snuggled in
close to her parents.

As she yawned and closed her eyes, she said,
'I hope tomorrow will be a lovely day
– the perfect day to have an adventure!'

*For Mum, Dad and Ross - **GD***

*For Hugh, Senan, Gabriel and Ronan - **SD***

First published 2019 by The O'Brien Press Ltd,
12 Terenure Road East, Rathgar, Dublin 6, D06 HD27, Ireland
Tel: +353 1 4923333; Fax: +353 1 4922777
E-mail: books@obrien.ie
Website: www.obrien.ie
Reprinted 2019.
The O'Brien Press is a member of Publishing Ireland.

Published in

DUBLIN
UNESCO
City of Literature

ISBN: 978-1-78849-050-4

8 7 6 5 4 3 2
22 21 20 19

Printed and bound in Poland by Białostockie Zakłady Graficzne S.A.
The paper in this book is produced using pulp from managed forests.

Where Are You, Puffling? receives financial assistance from the Arts Council

Life on the Skellig Islands